One T. Rex Over Easy

Read all the Carmen Sandiego™ Mysteries:

HASTA LA VISTA, BLARNEY

COLOR ME CRIMINAL

ONE T. REX OVER EASY

And coming soon:

THE COCOA COMMOTION

One T. Rex Over Easy

by Bonnie Bader & Tracey West

Illustrated by S. M. Taggart

*Based on the computer software
created by Brøderbund Software, Inc.*

HarperTrophy®
A Division of HarperCollinsPublishers

Harper Trophy® is a registered trademark of
HarperCollins Publishers Inc.

One T. Rex Over Easy

Library of Congress Cataloging-in-Publication Data
Bader, Bonnie.
    One T. rex over easy / by Bonnie Bader and Tracey West ; illustrated by
S. M. Taggart
        p.   cm.   (A Carmen Sandiego mystery)
    "Based on the computer software created by Brøderbund Software, Inc."
    Summary: ACME junior detectives Maya and Ben travel through time to
catch the elusive thief Carmen Sandiego, suspected of stealing a *Tyrannosaurus
rex* egg from the Cretaceous Period.
    ISBN 0-06-440679-2 (pbk.)
    [1. Time travel—Fiction. 2. Dinosaurs—Fiction. 3. Science fiction.]
I. West, Tracey.   II. Taggart, S. M., ill.   III. Title.   IV. Series.
PZ7.B1377On   1997   96-50364
[Fic]—dc21   CIP
                                                                      AC

Typography by Steve Scott
1   2   3   4   5   6   7   8   9   10
❖
First Edition

For my parents, two good eggs
—B.B.

For Lauren Noll, the girl who loves dinosaurs
—T.W.

Prologue
Alberta, Canada,
70 million years ago

The dinosaur opened his jaws wide and bit into his lunch with a loud crunch.

The juicy green fern tasted delicious to the *Ankylosaurus*. The peaceful plant-eater had certainly traveled far enough to find it. He had walked along the river all morning, searching for the tastiest young leaves he could find. The duckbills had eaten all the best plants closest to home.

The other *Ankylosaurs* were content to eat the stringy leaves that were left, but not him. This particular *Ankylosaurus* was young and rather brave. No predators had ever dared to bother with him. Hard plates covered his body like a suit of armor. Short, sharp spikes stuck out from both sides of his body. His powerful tail could be used like a club to break an attacker's leg. All of this protection had made him confident, which is why he had decided to journey into unfamiliar territory that morning.

The *Ankylosaurus* munched away and glanced lazily around the clearing he had discovered. A lush forest surrounded him. What a feast he could have there! Green trees, leafy ferns, and big, juicy flowers stretched on for miles.

The dinosaur's eyes settled on something a few yards to the right. It was a nest—a big, muddy nest. Leaves and twigs stuck out from all sides. It was too big to be a duckbill nest, or even an *ankylosaur* nest, for that matter. The nest could only have been made by one animal.

A *Tyrannosaurus rex.*

The *Ankylosaurus* sniffed the air. It was a *T. rex* nest all right. Still, there was no sign of one anywhere. If there was a mother guarding the nest, she was probably out hunting. Huge herds of duckbills were out grazing that time of day, and the *T. rex* would have no trouble finding one to fill its enormous appetite. The *Ankylosaurus* didn't think he had much to fear. After all, why would a *T. rex* try to bite through his hard armor if its belly was already full?

The *Ankylosaurus* moved closer to the nest. A single egg was resting in the center. The egg was the largest the dinosaur had ever seen—about as large as his own head.

Suddenly the *Ankylosaurus* heard a noise. It wasn't the thundering footsteps of an angry mother *T. rex;* it was a sound he had never heard before. It sounded like a thousand buzzing insects. The *Ankylosaurus* may have been brave, but he knew enough not to be an easy target. He moved away from the nest as quickly as he could on his short legs. The dinosaur hid behind a large rock and peered in the direction of the sound.

A strange animal was speeding toward the *T. rex* nest. The *Ankylosaurus* had never seen such a creature before. It didn't look at all like a dinosaur. It had a small head with a flat face—no snout. It carried itself upright, like a *T. rex*. But the strangest thing of all was that this animal appeared to be riding on the back of another animal—a shiny silver creature with two round legs that spun in circles.

The *Ankylosaurus* watched in amazement as the

animal paused in front of the nest. The loud buzzing noise stopped. The animal climbed off the back of the shiny silver beast. It climbed into the nest and grabbed the *T. rex* egg.

The *Ankylosaurus* blinked. This strange animal had no armor, no spikes to protect itself. It was either very brave or very stupid.

The ground began to shake. Another loud noise filled the clearing, and this time it *was* the thunderous footsteps of an angry *T. rex*. The dinosaur, whose head towered above the treetops, was running toward her nest.

The strange animal clutched the egg. It jumped back onto the silver beast and sped past the *T. rex*. The mother dinosaur bellowed and took off after the animal.

The strange animal raced into a strange-looking red box at the edge of the forest. The *T. rex* bent down to stick her head into the box.

Suddenly the box disappeared! The *Ankylosaurus* blinked again. The box had vanished right before his eyes. The strange animal and the *T. rex* egg were nowhere to be seen.

The *T. rex* let out an angry roar and stomped on the ground with her giant feet. Suddenly the *Ankylosaurus* wasn't feeling quite so brave anymore.

He decided it was time to head home. In fact, he decided it might be best to stick close to home from then on. At home he was safe from strange, buzzing animals and angry mother dinosaurs.

Besides, he told himself, the ferns in this clearing didn't taste all that great anyway.

1
ACME Headquarters, San Francisco, California, Present Day

"I can't believe The Chief wants to meet us on the thirteenth floor," Maya said as she pressed the elevator button.

"I can't believe it either," Ben replied. "I'm so excited, my hands are shaking!"

"You'd better make sure The Chief doesn't notice," Maya warned. "I don't want her to think we can't handle it."

Maya was usually pretty good at keeping her cool, but even *her* hands were shaking a little. The thirteenth floor was top secret—off-limits to all but the most expert ACME agents. Nine-year-old Maya and eleven-year-old Ben were the youngest detectives in the agency. Maya thought it would be years before they'd ever find out what was on the thirteenth floor. Now it was going to happen in just a few seconds.

The elevator came to a smooth stop, and the doors opened. Maya and Ben stepped out—and came face-to-face with a red steel door. A sign on the door read ABSOLUTELY NO ADMITTANCE WITHOUT PROPER CLEARANCE.

"What do we do now?" Ben asked.

Maya nodded toward a small screen mounted on the wall to the right of the door. "Watch this." She touched her right palm to the screen. A green light above the screen began to blink, and the word CLEARED appeared on the screen.

"The Chief had our palm prints on file, and she scanned them into the security center up here," Maya explained. "Try it."

Ben pressed his palm to the screen, and the green light flashed again. Maya and Ben stepped back as the red door slowly began to open inward.

The Chief was standing on the other side, in a small white room. "Greetings, gumshoes," she said. "You'd better move quickly. The door shuts automatically in ten seconds."

Maya and Ben obeyed, and the door slammed shut behind them.

The two gumshoes scanned the room. The Chief stood in the center wearing a neatly pressed blue suit; on her head, not a single short dark hair was out of place. The room was empty. There was no furniture, no doors, and no windows—just plain white walls.

"Is this all there is?" Ben asked. He sounded disappointed.

The Chief shook her head. "I thought you were sharper than that, Ben. This is a top-secret project. We've taken every precaution to keep it safe."

The Chief pulled a small metal microphone out of her pocket and spoke into it. "We're ready, Agent Thyme."

The wall in front of them slid open to reveal another room. This room was much larger, and was filled with wires, test tubes, and blinking lights. A small man with wiry gray hair emerged from the clutter and beckoned to them. His hair extended from his head as if it were electrically charged.

"Come in, come in," he called. "There is no time to lose."

The wall slid shut behind them as Maya and Ben followed The Chief into the strange laboratory.

"Agents, I'd like you to meet Otto Thyme. He's

the brains behind this project," The Chief said.

"What project?" Maya asked impatiently. "Chief, why are we here?"

Agent Thyme and The Chief exchanged glances. "We've got to show them, Thyme. We have no choice," The Chief said.

Thyme nodded and led them to a tall silver box in the corner of the lab. It looked like a phone booth without windows.

"Yes, yes, I suppose it is time," Thyme muttered. He cleared his throat. "Gumshoes, you are looking at a machine that has the ability to change the world—the Chronoskimmer 325i."

Ben gasped. "You mean—a time machine?"

Thyme nodded. "Exactly."

"No way!" Maya exclaimed. "Ben, how did you know?"

"Easy." Ben shrugged. "*Chronos* is an ancient Greek word meaning 'time.' It's used in lots of modern words, like chronology, chronicle—"

"Enough already," Maya interrupted. Her pride was stung a little. She was used to being the one with all the answers. "How did you get to be such a know-it-all?"

Ben smiled. "Easy. Those words were on my vocabulary test this week."

Maya groaned.

"Are you two finished?" The Chief asked. "We're on a very important case here."

"Sorry, Chief," Maya mumbled. She still had trouble remembering that her aunt Velma, who was so much fun at family parties, was all business when it came to her duties as ACME's chief.

"I'm sorry too," Ben said. "So, what is the case about, anyway?"

The Chief took a deep breath. She suddenly looked nervous and uncomfortable, which Maya thought was odd. She had seen The Chief in many moods—angry at an agent's mistake, happy when a case was solved—but she had never, ever seen her calm, cool aunt look nervous.

"It's Carmen, isn't it? She's up to her old tricks again," Maya said. Carmen Sandiego, the world's greatest thief and head of the criminal organization V.I.L.E. (Villains' International League of Evil), was always causing trouble for ACME.

"The truth is, I don't know what the case is about," The Chief said. "I had an . . . an experience one week ago that led me to believe that you two would be using the Chronoskimmer for an important mission today. If it hadn't been for my . . . experience, you two wouldn't be up here. Frankly,

I'm not convinced you're ready for the Chrono-skimmer yet."

Maya and Ben looked at each other. They knew what The Chief meant. They had a good track record capturing Carmen's V.I.L.E. agents, but on their last case Carmen had eluded them yet again.

Agent Thyme wrung his hands nervously. "Well, I'm not sure the Chronoskimmer is ready for *them*," he piped up. "I have been working on this machine since before you two were born. It wasn't supposed to be ready for another year. We haven't run enough tests yet."

Maya's stomach did a small flip. "Does that mean Ben and I will be the first ones to use it?"

"You'll be the first to use it on a mission for ACME," The Chief replied.

"Don't you have *any* idea what this is all about?" Ben asked. "Does Carmen have something to do with it?"

The Chief frowned. "That's the strange part. Carmen and her V.I.L.E. agents have been awfully quiet lately. We haven't gotten any reports on her in months. In fact, we've only heard one thing out of the ordinary. An agent in Alberta, Canada, received a report that a dinosaur was sighted roaming the wilderness. We dismissed the report as a hallucination. Agent

11

Thyme does have a theory, though. Thyme, why don't you tell them."

The gumshoes looked at the agent. He was patting the Chronoskimmer and whispering, "Don't worry now. Everything will be fine."

"Thyme!" The Chief said angrily. "Are you listening?"

The agent jumped. "Listening? Of course." He adjusted his glasses nervously. "As you know, Carmen worked as an agent at ACME before she left to form V.I.L.E. You may not know that she was my assistant. She helped me develop the Chronoskimmer." Thyme's eyes took on a faraway look. "Ah, Carmen. So vivacious, so brilliant. Who would have guessed that she would become so evil?"

"This is no time for reminiscing, Thyme," The Chief snapped. "Let's hear the rest of your theory."

"It sounds like he needs a *time-out*," Ben whispered to Maya. Maya giggled.

Thyme adjusted his wire glasses. "My theory. Of course," he said. "You see, I believe Carmen has developed her own time machine and that she's already used it to commit some outrageous theft."

"Oh, no!" Maya said. "So how is ACME supposed to stop her?"

The Chief stepped up to the Chronoskimmer.

"With this," she said. "If Thyme's theory is right, we'll need to go back in time in the Chronoskimmer and stop V.I.L.E.'s latest crime—before it happens."

"That's why you're here," Thyme said. "We need to show you how the Chronoskimmer works."

Maya and Ben stepped toward the time machine. The floor beneath them began to rumble and shake.

"Hey, what's going on?" Ben asked. "Is this another security feature?"

Another rumble shook the room. The Chief ducked as a piece of lab equipment flew off a shelf above her head.

"Negative, gumshoes," The Chief replied. "We seem to be experiencing an earthquake."

Ben pulled the Ultra-Secret Sender out of his knapsack. The Sender was a small rectangular gadget the size of a personal tape player, a combination computer/camcorder/videophone. Ben flipped open a panel to reveal a small computer screen. "I should be able to log into a seismic reading of the area," Ben said. After a few seconds he looked up from the screen. "That's odd. There are tremors recorded, but they're in a very small area just outside Headquarters. An earthquake would affect a much larger area than that."

13

Maya and Ben ran to a video monitor built into the wall of the lab. "Maybe there's something outside that's making the building shake, like a bulldozer or something," Maya said. "The videocams should show us what's going on."

Ben punched in some numbers on the monitor's keyboard. An image popped up on the screen. The street behind ACME Headquarters was filled with people running and screaming.

"Check this out," Ben said. "Something is definitely out there."

Maya, Agent Thyme, and The Chief gathered around the screen. Ben punched in more numbers. A view of the alley next to Headquarters popped up.

"Nothing here," Ben said. "Let's check the front."

Another picture filled the screen. It took Ben a second to register what it was.

It was an eye. A giant eye.

"What the . . ." The Chief muttered. "Ben, let's get a broader view."

Ben tapped some numbers on the keyboard. The videocam pulled back, and another image filled the screen. This image was even more incredible than the first. A giant dinosaur was stomping its huge legs.

"Is this a sci-fi movie or something?" Ben asked.

"No, Ben, it's real," Maya said, her voice rising. "It's a *Tyrannosaurus rex*, and it's attacking ACME Headquarters!"

2
ACME Headquarters, San Francisco, California, Present Day

"**A** T. rex!" Ben cried. Suddenly the dinosaur kicked one of its legs and took a huge chunk out of the side of the building. The floor shook violently. Ben's glasses flew off his face and slid across the lab's polished white floor. He scrambled after them.

"What are we going to do?" Maya asked, twirling one of her braids around her finger nervously. "We could be eaten alive!"

Then the T. rex swung its massive tail and hit the building. Test tubes crashed, sparks flew, and Maya, Ben, The Chief, and Agent Thyme were thrown to the ground.

"Cool!" Ben shouted, looking up admiringly at the image of the huge beast. All eyes in the room looked at Ben.

"I know you've been through a lot lately, gumshoe," The Chief said to him. "But this is not the time to get excited."

"Really, Ben," Maya said. "We're in *big* trouble here!"

Ben's face turned red. "I—I'm not excited, Chief," he stammered. "It's—it's just that there's a real live *T. rex* out there. I mean, those things have been dead for *years*. Sixty-five million years, to be exact."

Ben grabbed a nearby lab table and rose to his feet. "I went through a huge dinosaur phase when I was a little kid," he said. "I know all kinds of stuff about *Tyrannosaurus rex*. Its name means 'king of the tyrant lizards,' and it was the largest of the fearsome flesh-eating dinosaurs. It stood twenty feet tall on its powerful hind legs. It lived during the Late Cretaceous Period and its remains have been found in the northern United States, Canada—"

"And now it can be found here—right in San Francisco!" Maya interrupted. Then she turned and looked at The Chief, who was staring at the video monitor.

"Aunt—" Maya began, before correcting herself. "I mean, Chief, is this some kind of virtual-reality game, or is all this really happening?"

The room shook again, and Maya knew that this was all too real.

"If I may say something," Agent Thyme spoke up. "I think I know what has happened."

Maya and Ben turned and looked at the small man. In all the excitement, they had almost forgotten that the agent was in the room with them.

"As I said before, Carmen and V.I.L.E. have probably developed their own time machine. It does make sense. She was so clever, so smart, so—"

"Agent Thyme!" The Chief snapped. "Enough about that thief! You said you had figured something out. Well, what is it?"

"I've got it!" Ben shouted out suddenly. "Carmen. Time machine. *T. rex*." He was so excited that he could barely get the words out.

Maya had figured it out too. She put her hand on her friend's shoulder. "What Ben's trying to say, Chief, is that Carmen must have used her machine to go back in time—to steal a dinosaur from the past!"

"Impressive, gumshoes," The Chief said, a faint smile forming on her lips. "But it was probably one of her accomplices who did the actual stealing."

Maya looked up at the video monitor again. The *T. rex* was standing still. It looked like it was pondering its next move. A chill ran down Maya's spine.

"But why would a V.I.L.E. agent go back in time and bring a dinosaur here?" Maya wondered aloud.

"I don't think it's really possible that one of Carmen's henchpeople actually brought that thing here," Ben said, pointing to the video monitor. "I mean, that thing is huge. It's more likely he or she stole a *T. rex* egg and brought it back through time. What we're looking at is that egg all grown up!

"However," he continued, "scientists have never been able to prove that the *T. rex* laid eggs. Still, it's the only theory that makes sense."

Agent Thyme had a sad look on his face. He stared at the Chronoskimmer and shook his head. "So inventive. So cunning. So—"

"Perhaps you would like to sit down," The Chief said to Agent Thyme, ushering him to a chair.

The Chief walked over to the Chronoskimmer and touched it. "Carmen has really done it this time," she mused. "She has really done it."

Maya and Ben walked over and joined her at the machine. The Chief had that worried look on her face again.

"Gumshoes," The Chief said, still staring at the time machine, "we have a case here, and it's a big one."

This time Maya's stomach did a *big* flip. "What do you want Ben and me to do, Chief?" she asked, although she had an idea.

"You two are going to have to pay a little visit to our *T. rex*'s home," The Chief said.

"I knew it!" Maya cried. "We're going to travel through time!"

"Y-you want us to take that thing back home?" Ben stammered.

"Yeah, right, Ben," Maya said. "We're just going to go out there, take it by the hand, and say, 'Time to go now.' Get real, Ben!"

Ben blushed. "I—I didn't think so."

"No, gumshoes," The Chief said. "Your mission is to go back in time and stop Carmen's hench-person *before* the egg is stolen."

Maya and Ben nodded. They had their orders, but they weren't sure exactly how they were supposed to carry them out. This case was unlike any other they had tackled before.

"So you mean we'll be going back to the Late Cretaceous Period?" Ben wanted to know.

The Chief nodded.

"But exactly *where* in the Cretaceous Period should we go?" Ben asked.

"I know!" Maya spoke up. "Remember that report you dismissed, Chief, the one about a dinosaur being sighted in Alberta, Canada? That's it! That's our clue," she said, typing furiously into the Ultra-Secret Sender.

"Scientists discovered *T. rex* remains there in the early 1900s," Maya reported. "In fact, as early as the 1870s scientists thought there were dinosaur remains in Alberta, just waiting to be dug up! Carmen must have figured that Alberta was a sure bet for finding a *T. rex*."

"Right!" Ben said. "I'll bet Carmen's agent stole the egg in Canada, and Carmen's been raising the *T. rex* there ever since. That would explain that dinosaur sighting."

"Then I say we know where to go," Maya concluded. "Alberta, Canada. Late Cretaceous Period."

Once they had figured out their destination, Maya and Ben turned and looked at Agent Thyme. They knew *where* they were going, but they did not know *how* to get there.

22

The Chief cleared her throat. "That's your cue, Agent Thyme."

The agent snapped to attention. "Ah yes, now, where was I?"

"You were about to show our two junior detectives here how to work this little contraption of yours," The Chief said, gently patting the Chronoskimmer.

"You mean they're actually going to operate my time machine?" Agent Thyme said. "As I said before, Chief, we still need to run more tests."

"There have been more than enough tests!" The Chief snapped. "You know the Chronoskimmer is safe. We must activate it immediately!"

Agent Thyme opened up the time machine's door and ushered Maya and Ben inside. Two shiny metal seats were positioned in front of a control panel. Agent Thyme pointed to a set of buttons and a keyboard on the lower right-hand side of the panel. "This first button is your travel button," he began. "First you enter the spatial coordinates—that's the place you want. Then you enter the temporal coordinates—that's the time period you want. It's as simple as that.

"And finally, all your information is in here," Agent Thyme said, tapping the control panel. "This is your communication window. It's your phone, camcorder, fax, translator, and decoder, as well as your access to the Internet and the ACME CrimeNet database," he said proudly.

"Gee, that sounds familiar," Maya said with a giggle. It had all the functions of the Ultra-Secret Sender.

"Well, that's all. You should be off," The Chief said. She reached down and shook Maya's and Ben's hands. "Good luck, gumshoes." And with that, she walked out of the Chronoskimmer and shut the door.

Maya and Ben were alone. And they were about to embark on the biggest case of their careers. They gave each other a nervous smile. Maya switched on the TRAVEL button. Ben typed in: SPATIAL COORDINATES: ALBERTA, CANADA. TEMPORAL COORDINATES: LATE CRETACEOUS PERIOD.

The machine shook and the lights dimmed. They were off.

3
Alberta, Canada,
70 Million Years Ago

Lights flashed, and a soft whirring sound filled the air. Ben sucked in his breath and grasped the armrests of his chair. He glanced over at Maya. She, too, was clutching her chair.

Ben looked at the Chronoskimmer's control panel. The time periods flashed by: Cretaceous, Jurassic, Triassic. Wait a second, what was going on?

"Oh my gosh, Maya!" Ben exclaimed. "We've gone too far!"

Maya looked at the control panel. Ben was right. They were in the Triassic Period. "We've got to do something, Ben!" she said, panic growing in her voice.

The Chronoskimmer shook, and Maya and Ben

were thrown forward in their seats. Ben looked at the screen again. It read: CURRENT LOCATION: ALBERTA, CANADA. CURRENT TIME PERIOD: JURASSIC PERIOD. Maybe the time machine is making some sort of adjustment, he thought. They waited a few minutes, but nothing else happened. They were stuck.

"Maybe we should get out here," Maya suggested.

"No way," Ben said. "If we get out now, we'll never find the *T. rex*—it wasn't alive during the Jurassic Period."

Maya was trying to remain calm. "Let's try contacting Agent Thyme," she suggested, typing some information into the control panel's keyboard. "He said that this should function like our Ultra-Secret Sender, so let's give it a try."

A few seconds later a fuzzy image of Agent Thyme appeared on the screen. "Thank goodness!" Maya cried. "Agent Thyme, something's not right. We've made it to Alberta, but we've gone back too far."

Agent Thyme scratched his head. "I told The Chief more tests were needed. Well, you'll just have to try to program it again."

Since they were already at the correct geographical place, all they had to do was punch in the correct temporal coordinate—Late Cretaceous Period. And once *that* was done, all they had to do was cross their fingers.

The time machine whirred back to life. They took off and landed quietly a few seconds later. Maya looked at the control panel. CURRENT LOCATION: ALBERTA, CANADA. CURRENT TIME PERIOD: LATE CRETACEOUS PERIOD. They had made it!

Maya unbuckled her seat belt and jumped out of her chair. "Come on, Ben," she said. "Let's go!"

Ben got up and followed Maya out of the time machine. The first thing they noticed was that the air was warm and mild.

"I thought Canada was supposed to be cold," Ben said, taking off his windbreaker and putting it into his knapsack.

"If you were to come here in our time, especially during the winter, it *would* be cold. Freezing, in fact," Maya said. She smiled smugly. Ben might know about dinosaurs, but she was still the geography expert, no matter what year it was. "Remember, this is the Cretaceous Period. The climate was different back then—the world was a much warmer place. In fact, *most* things were different back then."

Ben nodded, eager to hear what she was going to say next.

"Believe it or not," Maya continued as they walked along, "scientists think that all the continents were once joined together. They were one big land mass surrounded by an enormous sea. For a long time dinosaurs could walk over the land connections between continents."

"You mean they could walk from North America to Asia?" Ben asked in disbelief.

"Well, it would be a long walk, but it could be done," Maya said, shrugging. "Eventually the continents started drifting apart, and as they did, shallow water covered a lot of North America, Europe, and southern Asia."

"That's amazing!" Ben said.

Maya nodded.

"Hey!" Ben exclaimed, stopping in his tracks. "What's with all the palm trees? I thought we were in Canada, not Hawaii."

Maya laughed. "They're not palm trees. They're called cycads."

Maya took Ben over to one of the trees. Its leathery, fernlike leaves grew in a circle at the end of the stem. As she reached over to touch a leaf, something behind the tree moved. It was a dinosaur! Short, sharp spikes stuck out from both sides of its body. And it looked like its heavy, spiked tail could take the two gumshoes out with a single swipe!

"Uh, Ben," Maya said, slowly backing away. "I—I don't know for sure, but I could swear that dinosaur over there is staring at us!"

Ben laughed.

"What's so funny?" Maya asked, growing angry with Ben. "That's not a cute little furry animal over there. It's a *dinosaur*. As in, a dinosaur that could *eat* us!"

"Don't worry, Maya," Ben said. "It's just an *Ankylosaurus*. He's a plant-eater. And he's probably just curious. After all, he's probably never seen a human before."

Maya breathed a sigh of relief.

They walked on in silence for a while. Frogs and lizards scampered at their feet. Over in the distance, Ben pointed out herds of *Edmontosauruses*, a kind of duckbill, feeding on pine needles.

"This place is amazing!" Ben said after a while. "Do you realize we're the first humans to set eyes on this?"

"We might not be the first—Carmen's agent could have been here before us, remember?" Maya said. "Anyway, we can't forget we've got a job to do. Our first order of business should be trying to find the agent—and the *T. rex* egg, if there is one."

"Let's start looking," Ben said.

Maya and Ben made their way across the muddy terrain. They saw prints in all shapes and sizes. Suddenly Maya noticed something on the ground that didn't seem to fit in with their present surroundings, yet it looked very familiar to her. She dropped to her knees, her face very close to the mud.

"Are you okay, Maya?" Ben asked. "What are you doing down there?"

"Look at this," she said, pointing to what she had found.

Ben knelt down and saw a long ridged track in the mud. "Motorcycle tires," he concluded.

"Right," Maya agreed. "And since motorcycles weren't around during the time of the dinosaurs, it can mean only one thing!"

"That we're on the trail of one of Carmen's henchpeople!" Ben finished.

"Let's follow it!" Maya said. And they started to run alongside it.

The track led them to what looked like a big, muddy nest made of leaves and twigs.

"Would you look at that," Ben said. "A nest. And from the size of it, I'd guess it belongs to a *T. rex*. I guess they lay eggs after all," he said.

"It sure looks that way," Maya agreed. "But

let's take a closer look. Hopefully the egg is still there."

They walked over to the nest and peered inside. It was empty. They were too late.

"We missed him!" Maya said, stamping her foot. A spray of mud shot up and splattered her in the face. "Or her," she added.

Maya sighed, and wiped her face with the sleeve of her T-shirt. "Well, I guess we have to try to find a clue that tells us where the hench-person went next," she said.

"And while we're looking for clues, I might as well try to find something to eat," Ben said. "Time travel makes me hungry!"

"I doubt we're going to find a hot-dog stand around here," Maya said, rummaging through her backpack for some food. "Here, eat this," she said, pulling out a granola bar.

"That's *it*?" Ben asked, suddenly remembering that he didn't have anything better in his pack. They had left ACME in such a hurry that they hadn't had time to pack food.

"Maybe there *is* something edible around here," Maya said, pointing to the plants surrounding them. "Why don't we pick up some plants and seeds, take them back, and run some tests in the

Chronoskimmer's lab? We're bound to find *something* we can eat."

As they were gathering up the vegetation, Maya noticed some huge footprints in the mud. "Hey, Ben," she called. "Come over here and check this out. These prints belong to one big critter!"

Suddenly the ground shook. The two young detectives looked up just in time to see a huge beast storming toward them. The animal stopped for a moment and let out a terrifying roar. It was the mother *T. rex*, and she was returning home.

Everything was happening so quickly that Maya and Ben didn't know what to do. But what they did know was that they had to get out of there—and fast!

They raced through the forest as swiftly as they could. But with each step, the *T. rex* was gaining on them.

"We're dinosaur meat!" Ben shouted. "The *T. rex* will eat us alive!"

"Not if I can help it." Maya turned around and threw her granola bar straight at the dinosaur. Startled, the *T. rex* sniffed the strange object. That was just the distraction they needed. Maya and Ben cut a path to the left and were quickly out of sight.

"That was a close one!" Ben said once they were safely back inside the Chronoskimmer. "I bet the missing egg belongs to that *T. rex*. And she probably thinks we are the ones who stole it!"

"Well, let's get to work and try to figure out who did," Maya said.

"The first thing we should do is try to find out which V.I.L.E. agents ride motorcycles," Ben said as he typed the specifics on the control panel's keyboard.

Soon the information came up:

ROSA SARROSAS-ARROZ. RED HAIR, BROWN EYES, HAS SCAR ON LEFT INDEX FINGER. HOBBY: CROQUET. FOOD: CHINESE. VEHICLE: MOTORCYCLE.

NICK BRUNCH. BLACK HAIR, GREEN EYES, MUSTACHE. LIKES JEWELRY. HOBBY: MOUNTAIN CLIMBING. FOOD: MEXICAN. VEHICLE: MOTORCYCLE.

KATHERINE DRIB. BROWN HAIR, BLUE EYES, TATTOO OF EAGLE ON LEFT BICEPS. HOBBY: MOUNTAIN CLIMBING. FOOD: SEAFOOD. VEHICLE: MOTORCYCLE.

DINAH SORE. BLOND HAIR, BLUE EYES,
DINOSAUR EXPERT AT LOCAL MUSEUM.
HOBBY: STAMP COLLECTING. FOOD: JUNK FOOD.
VEHICLE: MOTORCYCLE.

"Four agents in all," Maya concluded.

"Of course! Dinah!" Ben shouted. "She's the dinosaur expert—it must be her!"

"Let's not jump to any conclusions," Maya said. "According to her dossier, Dinah is an academic. She probably spends her days in a dusty museum—she doesn't sound like the adventurous, time-traveling type. We'll need more clues before we can pin this on her."

"I need a break," Ben complained. "I'm *starving*! Let's test this food."

One by one they started placing the leaves, flowers, and seeds in the Chronoskimmer's analyzer. The first couple of items were indigenous to the area, and some were perfectly safe to eat.

"That's strange," Maya said, looking at the results of a seed they had just tested. "According to the analyzer, this seed is from a calvaria tree. And calvaria trees are found only on the island of Mauritius, not in Alberta, Canada!"

"Island of Delicious?" Ben asked.

Rosa Sarrosas-Arroz

Katherine Drib

Nick Brunch

Dinah Sore

"No, *Mauri*tius!"

"Then that's it!" Ben shouted. "That's our clue. The V.I.L.E. henchperson must have received it as a clue for where to meet Carmen and dropped it!"

Then his face fell. "Now we know *where* to go, but we don't know *when* to go."

But Maya was smiling. She held a printout in her hand. "I think this will help us. There are only a few old calvaria trees left on the island of Mauritius. That's because the dodo bird, which is now extinct, used to eat the tree's fruit, grind up the seeds, and pass them out in droppings. The seeds can't grow without this happening, and since the dodoes aren't around anymore, there aren't too many calvaria trees left." Maya stopped and took a deep breath.

"So when were dodoes alive?" Ben asked impatiently.

Maya's face fell. "It's hard to say exactly. They lived on the island for thousands of years. It wasn't until European settlers came in the fifteenth and sixteenth centuries that they became endangered."

"We can't spend thousands of years on Mauritius," Ben said. "Let's keep looking through this stuff. Maybe something else will help us narrow down the date."

Once again Maya and Ben went through the vegetation they had collected. Suddenly Maya came across something white in her pile. For a moment she thought it was some sort of bud, but then she realized it was a very small piece of crumpled paper. Very carefully she unfolded it. On the paper was some very small writing. Maya whipped out her magnifying glass and read: "Tasman."

"As in Tasmanian devil?" Ben asked.

Maya shrugged. "I don't know how this fits in. What does the Tasmanian devil have in common with the island of Mauritius?"

"You tell me," Ben shot back. "I'd never even heard of Mauritius until you mentioned it just now."

"I know!" Maya finally said. "Tasman was a Dutch explorer who discovered the island of Tasmania. Mauritius is an island west of Tasmania in the Pacific Ocean. Maybe *that's* the connection."

Ben typed this information into the control panel. "You're onto something," he said. "According to the computer, Tasman's first stop in his journey to Tasmania was the island of Mauritius! He left Mauritius sometime around October 8, 1642. Should we give it a try?"

Maya thought hard for a minute. "Well, we could either try to go back a while in the Cretaceous Period and wait for Carmen's henchperson to arrive, or follow them to Mauritius."

"Come to think of it," said Ben, "I think we

would *save* time by going to the next place. At least we have a date in Mauritius. Who knows how long ago the egg was stolen? We'd have to go back weeks to make sure to be here at the right time. Let's take a vote."

Suddenly the ground shook. Maya looked out through the peephole. The mother *T. rex* had found them! "Uh, Ben," she said. "I vote we leave the Cretaceous Period—right away!"

"You don't have to convince me!" Ben said. "Next stop: Mauritius, October 8, 1642!"

When I hatched my plan to steal a T. rex *egg, I never thought ACME would be smart enough to go back in time and try to stop me. But those young detectives are clever, very clever.*

And my agent was careless, very careless—dropping clues like that. But it doesn't matter. Those overly enthusiastic amateurs will never stop me from unleashing my Cretaceous creature on the world. I am Carmen Sandiego, the greatest thief of any *era. And I've got all of history to hide in. Those two will never be able to find me!*

4

Mauritius,
October 8, 1642

"**O**uch!" Ben yelled. The Chronoskimmer had just landed with a jarring thump, causing him to bang his head on the control panel.

"Agent Thyme never guaranteed us any smooth landings," Maya said. "Come on, you'll feel better once we're breathing that fresh ocean air."

"That's easy for you to say," Ben replied, rubbing the top of his blond head.

Maya and Ben stepped out of the Chronoskimmer. Bright sunlight and an ocean breeze greeted them.

"I'm glad it's cooler than it was in Alberta," Ben remarked. "It's just about perfect here!"

"The weather is always pretty nice on Mauritius,"

Maya replied. "It's a tropical island, so the temperature stays about the same all year long. It doesn't get too hot or too cold."

Ben surveyed the land around him. The Chronoskimmer had landed on the island's coast. Lush trees and flowers lined the sandy beach. In the distance, some of the forest had been cut away to make room for a settlement of wooden houses. A large sailing ship was docked alongside the houses.

"Is that a Dutch settlement?" Ben asked. "Maybe that's where we'll find Tasman—and Carmen's henchperson."

Maya nodded. "Maybe. It looks like we'll have to hike up there. But first let's brush up on Mauritius."

Maya stepped back into the Chronoskimmer and punched in MAURITIUS—HISTORY.

"It says here that the Portuguese were the first to discover Mauritius, in 1511," Maya said. "The island was uninhabited. The Portuguese didn't stay for long, and the next people to come to Mauritius were the Dutch, led by Vice Admiral Van Warwyck, in 1598. Van Warwyck landed on the southeast coast of the island. The Dutch used Mauritius as a supply base until 1638, when they decided to settle here."

Ben punched some numbers into the Chrono-skimmer's navigator. "We're on the southeast coast of the island, all right," he said. "We must be in the right place."

"Let's just hope we're in the right time, too— in time to catch Carmen's agent," Maya said. "Let's go!"

"I'm right behind you," Ben said. "It looks like Thyme equipped the Chronoskimmer with a portable translator. I'd better grab it—unless you've learned how to speak Dutch since our last case."

Maya grimaced. "Very funny. But that's a good idea. I'll take a printout of the Mauritius information in case we need it."

Back on the sunny beach, Ben made a beeline for the trees. "Let's keep out of sight so Carmen's agent doesn't see us," he suggested.

"Okay," Maya said. She looked at the printout. "According to this, we don't have to worry about encountering any strange animals. Except maybe for—"

"Aaaaah!" Ben screamed as a small, furry creature leaped out in front of him.

Maya laughed. "Except maybe for monkeys."

The monkey chattered at Ben, then swung away on its long tail.

"We *must* be in the right time period," Maya continued. "Monkeys aren't native to Mauritius. Portuguese sailors brought them here as pets, and the population later grew and became wild. They fed on dodo eggs. In fact, some scientists blame the monkeys for the extinction of the dodo bird."

"Is that why the dodoes died out?" Ben asked.

Maya scanned the printout. "That's part of the reason. It says here that the Dutch settlers killed the dodoes for food too."

Ben continued through the trees. "Speaking of dodoes, do you think we'll get to see one?"

"Probably," Maya said. "There were a lot of them on the island in 1642." She stopped in front of a tall tree with a silver trunk.

Ben stopped, puzzled, then noticed an odd-looking brown seed on the ground. "Hey, there's another calvaria seed!" he cried. "Is this a calvaria tree?"

"It sure is," Maya said. "This looks like a whole forest of them. You'd never see that today."

"I never thought about it, but I guess trees can become endangered too," Ben said, looking up at the canopy of leaves overhead. "At least we got to see them. I really hope we get to see a dodo bird while we're here too."

Maya smiled. "Your wish just might come true. Watch out!"

"What do you mean?" Ben asked. He went to take a step forward—and almost stepped on something.

"Hey!" he shouted. A large, plump bird with a curved beak was staring at him with its two round blue eyes.

"You were too busy looking up at the sky to notice that a dodo bird was right at your feet!" Maya said, laughing.

Ben knelt down and looked at the bird. It took a step toward him, and its round body swayed. "What a cool-looking bird," he said. "Isn't she scared? How come she didn't fly away?"

"Dodoes can't fly," Maya reminded him. "See those tiny wings? Do they look like they could support such a big body?"

"I guess not." Ben looked at Maya. "That's probably why they were so easy to catch," he said. "I can't believe there are no more left on Earth. That's so sad."

Maya put her hand on Ben's shoulder. "We're really lucky that we got to see one in person," she said softly. "I wish we had more time, but—"

Ben stood up. "I know. We're almost at the Dutch

settlement." He turned to the bird. "Take care, dodo. Stay away from monkeys and hungry sailors."

Ben and Maya continued walking quietly. Soon the trees cleared, and they saw a cluster of crude wooden houses in front of them.

"We're here," Ben said. "Any sign of Carmen's agent?"

"Not that I can see," Maya replied. "I guess we'll have to ask around."

Ben glanced down at his jeans and sneakers. "Is that such a good idea? We don't exactly look like seventeenth-century Dutch sailors."

Maya shrugged. "We don't have much of a choice. We'll think of something."

The gumshoes stepped out of the trees. Most of the settlers were down by the water, at the sailing ship. There was one man, however, sitting on a worn wooden barrel outside a small house. His long red hair was pulled back in a ponytail. Cold blue eyes stared from his tanned, lined face. He wore a white shirt, and brown pants tucked into leather boots. His weathered hands were carving what looked like a monkey out of a piece of driftwood.

Maya and Ben approached the man. Ben pulled the Sender out of his backpack and flicked on the translator.

"Excuse me, sir, but we're looking for—"

The man leaned forward and poked Ben's chest. "You don't feel like a hallucination."

Ben frowned. "What do you mean?"

"As soon as I saw you two coming, I figured you must be another hallucination, as all I've been seeing lately are strange figures roaming about," the man said. "I tried to tell my captain, but all he could say was 'Frederick Klaver, you've been at sea too long. It happens to the best of men.'"

Maya stepped forward. "Mr. Klaver, you're not hallucinating," she explained. "We're from a—a neighboring island, one you haven't discovered yet. Can you please tell us about those other strange figures you saw?"

"They're friends of ours," Ben joined in. "We really need to find them."

Klaver's eyebrows furrowed. "If I tell you, will you go away? I've had enough hallucinations for one day."

Maya smiled. "We'll be gone before you know it!"

Klaver beckoned Maya and Ben closer. "Well then," he began. "'Twas yesterday that a strange woman in red appeared—"

"Carmen!" Ben whispered.

The sailor continued. "The woman gave a rolled-up parchment and a silver coin to the ship's steward on Abel Tasman's ship, with instructions to keep them safe for her. Then she disappeared. Then not an hour ago, another woman arrived— in breeches, no less! Just like you are, young lady," he said to Maya, pointing to her shorts. "This woman came to me, just as you did, asking about the woman in red. I sent her to Tasman's steward."

"The V.I.L.E. agent!" Ben shouted. "At least we know it's a woman. That rules out Nick Brunch."

"Whoever it is," Maya said, "she must be having the same trouble we're having with our time machine. She probably missed a rendezvous with Carmen yesterday, and Carmen left her instructions for their next meeting."

Ben jumped up. "There might still be time to catch her!" He grabbed Frederick Klaver's hand and shook it. "Thanks a lot! You'll never see us again—we promise."

The two gumshoes ran off in the direction of Tasman's ship. The shore was crowded with sailors preparing for their voyage.

"How will we find the steward? Or Carmen's agent?" Ben wondered aloud. "This place is swarming with sailors."

"At least they're too busy to notice us," Maya said. She scanned the crowd, and spotted a small man writing in a leather book.

"That must be the steward," Maya said. "The steward is responsible for the record-keeping on a ship."

Maya and Ben approached the sailor. He was only slightly taller than Ben, and rounder and less weathered-looking than Frederick Klaver.

"Excuse me, sir, but we're looking for someone," Ben said, after switching on the translator again. "We understand she might have just met with you."

The steward narrowed his eyes at Ben. "Do you mean that strange creature with the breeches and the cap pulled down over her face?" he asked. "I might have seen her. Of course, a gold piece would help me remember."

Ben sighed in frustration. "We don't have any gold pieces. Can't you help us?"

Maya chimed in. "I hear it's good luck to perform a good deed before a long voyage."

The steward raised an eyebrow. "Is that so? All right, then. Yes, I did see your friend. I gave her the piece of parchment the woman in red gave me and she ran away. But I forgot to give her this."

The man held up a silver coin with the profile of a man on it and writing in strange letters. He smiled. "I guess I'll have to keep it."

"Can I see that?" Maya asked.

The steward yanked his hand back.

"I'll give it back," Maya said. "I promise."

Maya and Ben examined the coin. "That looks like Russian writing." She examined it closer. "There are some numbers, too: '1801.'"

Ben turned to the steward. "What about the parchment? What did it say?"

The sailor pulled a piece of paper out of his jacket pocket. "It was a map," he said. "I was curious, so I made a copy. I thought it might be a route to the Spice Islands. But it doesn't look like any land I've ever seen."

Maya pulled a pencil from her pocket. "Can I please make a tracing?"

The man hesitated, then handed Maya the map. "I must be going soft in the head. It's just that you've got me missing my little girl back home. . . ." His voice drifted off.

Maya finished tracing the map and returned it to the steward. "Thank you, sir," she said. "What about our friend? Did you see which way she went?"

"Aye." The steward nodded. He pointed toward the shore. "She went back to her vessel. There she is now."

Maya and Ben quickly turned toward the shore, where a large box jutted out of the sand. It looked like the Chronoskimmer, but it was bigger, and it was red, not silver. A figure in jeans and a leather jacket was running toward the box, her back toward the agents. A cap covered her hair.

"It's the V.I.L.E. time machine!" Ben yelled. "Stop her!"

The gumshoes pushed through the throngs of busy sailors and took off after the agent. Maya ran as fast as she could. She was catching up! But suddenly she went flying, and landed facedown in the sand. Ben tripped and tumbled after her.

Maya sat up and looked behind her. A round bird stared at her blankly. She had been tripped up by a dodo bird!

"She's getting away!" Ben yelled.

Maya whirled around. The red box was shaking. There was a whirring noise, and then the box vanished into thin air.

Carmen's agent had slipped from their grasp!

5

Siberia, Russia, 1806

"**I** can't believe we missed her! We were so close!" Ben said. He sat down, breathless, on the floor of the Chronoskimmer.

"We'll get her next time," Maya said. "But we'll have to be careful. Now she knows we're on her trail."

Ben nodded. "You're right. Let's think about the clues we found. We have to figure out where to go next."

"Well, that coin the steward showed me was definitely a Russian coin. And 1801 must be the year. That narrows down the time period, and the country," said Maya.

"That's great, but where should we go?" Ben

asked. "Russia's a pretty big place."

Maya took the copy of the map from her pocket. "I have a hunch." She pulled up a map of northern Russia on the control panel and compared the two.

"Take a look," she said, pointing to the maps. "Carmen's map showed the northern coast of Siberia, along the Laptev Sea."

Ben peered closer. "What's that dot there?"

"That dot appears at the mouth of the Lena River," Maya said. "But why would Carmen's agent want to go there?"

Ben thought for a minute. "This might be a crazy idea, but hear me out. So far we've been led to dinosaurs and dodo birds—both extinct animals. It's starting to form a pattern. Maybe Siberia was home to an extinct animal too."

"Of course! You're a genius, Ben," Maya exclaimed, and began typing into the keyboard. "I'm searching for any record of an extinct animal living in the area around 1801."

The Chronoskimmer was quiet for several minutes, until Maya cried out, "I've got something! But it's not what we were thinking."

"What do you mean?" Ben asked.

"The Lena River wasn't home to an extinct

animal during that time period—but the remains of an extinct animal *were* discovered there."

Ben leaned over her shoulder and read aloud from the screen: " 'In 1799 a Russian ivory collector named Ossip Shumakhov discovered a giant mass embedded in ice at the mouth of the Lena River. By 1801 the mass had dislodged from the earth, and Shumakhov was able to see what it was—the remains of a woolly mammoth, preserved in the ice.' "

Ben turned to Maya. "It fits," he said. "Visiting the site of a discovery of an extinct animal is almost as good as seeing that animal in person."

"Let's try it. Siberia, 1801," Maya said, reaching for the control panel.

Ben grabbed her hand.

"Wait one second," Ben said. "I'm no geography expert, but I do know that Siberia is one of the coldest regions on the planet. We can't go walking around there without coats, gloves, boots, scarves—"

"Okay, you've got a point," Maya interrupted. "But what can we do? Yul B. Gowen usually sets us up with all the supplies we need. But he hasn't even been born yet!"

Yul was ACME's travel agent. Not only did he

get them wherever they needed to go, but he also provided them with supplies and advice.

"I know," Ben said, his voice rising. "All we have to do is program the Chronoskimmer for ACME Headquarters, back in the present. We can find Yul, get some warm clothes, and then go to Siberia."

"But won't we risk missing the V.I.L.E. agent?" Maya asked.

Ben shook his head. "No. Don't you see? We can set the Chronoskimmer for any time we want."

Maya sighed. "This time-travel stuff makes my head hurt. But I think I understand. Even if we spend a few minutes with Yul B. Gowen, we can still set the Chronoskimmer to arrive in Siberia before the V.I.L.E. agent gets there—if we're lucky."

"Right!" Ben said. "So let's make a detour to the present."

Maya programmed the coordinates, and the Chronoskimmer began to whir. The time machine landed with a thud.

"Not again!" Ben said. The machine shook violently.

"What's going on?" Maya yelled. She and Ben stepped out of the Chronoskimmer and into the lobby of ACME Headquarters. The lobby walls were moving.

"It must be the *T. rex*!" Ben cried. "The attack is getting worse!"

Maya grabbed Ben's hand. "We've got to find Yul—and fast!"

The gumshoes ran up to the second floor and into Yul B. Gowen's office.

The ACME travel agent was waiting for them at the door. "When The Chief told me about the case you two were on, I thought you might need a hand," Yul said. "It's good to see you. What do you need?"

A loud rumble shook the office.

"What we really need is to find Carmen's agent and return that egg," Maya said. "But right now we'll settle for some cold-weather gear. We're going to Siberia."

"Some lunch would be nice too," Ben added.

Maya nudged him.

"I can't help it," Ben said. "Those Cretaceous plants just weren't very filling."

"Coming right up," Yul said. Maya watched as he disappeared into a supply closet. She was always amazed at what he was able to pull out of there.

Yul emerged a few seconds later carrying insulated parkas, two pairs of boots, and thermal mittens. "These are the best I can do on short notice," he said. He went to his desk and handed Ben a small, lightweight pack.

"As far as lunch goes, the best I can offer is an emergency rations kit," Yul said. "Granola bars, dried fruit, and some dried soup mix you can reconstitute in water. In Siberia you might want to try melting snow. You should find plenty of it there."

"We've had good luck with granola so far," Maya said, remembering the mother *T. rex*. "We'll take it!"

Another rumble rattled the office.

Yul shook his head. "It's that poor *T. rex* again," he said. "I'm worried about it. The National Guard has been called in. I hope the frightened creature doesn't get hurt!"

Maya turned to Ben. "We'd better get back to the Chronoskimmer."

When Maya and Ben reached the lobby, the time machine was bouncing all over the lobby floor, thanks to the *T. rex*'s tremors. Maya and Ben jumped in and Ben plugged in the new information. SPATIAL COORDINATES: LENA RIVER, SIBERIA. TEMPORAL COORDINATES: 1801.

This time the Chronoskinner landed softly.

"Maybe we landed in a snowbank," Ben said.

"Speaking of snow, we should get our gear on,"

Maya said. "The average temperature in Siberia is between zero and thirty-nine degrees Fahrenheit, depending on the season."

The gumshoes quickly bundled up. Only their eyes were visible under their parka hoods.

"I hope we won't have to go on another chase," Ben said. "I don't think I can move very fast under all this insulation."

Maya and Ben stepped out underneath the cold blue sky. Once again the Chronoskimmer had landed them next to an ocean, but this coastline looked quite different. Instead of sand and green trees, a snowy blanket covered the ground and blocks of ice jutted out of the earth into a river-bank.

"We're here—at the Lena River," Maya said. "The ice is starting to thaw. It must be spring."

Ben looked around and spotted a small village in the distance. "Where do we go now?"

"North—toward the mouth of the river," Maya said. "It shouldn't be far."

Twenty minutes later, Ben was feeling tired. And hungry. "Not far? What's your definition of far?" he called out to Maya.

"Don't be so impatient," Maya said. She pointed to a spot up ahead. "I think we've made it."

A crowd of people in hooded fur coats was gathered around the riverbank. Ben switched on the translator. One man was giving orders to the others. Ben approached him.

"Are you Ossip Shumakhov?"

The man's eyes widened. "That scoundrel! Certainly not. I am Mikhail Adams, of the Russian Academy of Sciences. I am here on a very important scientific discovery." He gestured in the direction of the riverbank.

Maya and Ben moved closer to the bank. Large brown bones were protruding from the melting ice. Some of the bones were taller than the gumshoes.

"It's the woolly mammoth!" Maya cried. She turned to Adams. "But I don't understand. I thought this was Shumakhov's discovery."

"Shumakhov did find the mammoth—but that was five years ago," Adams said. "I have only just been informed of its existence."

Maya and Ben looked at each other.

"Five years?" Maya said.

"The Chronoskimmer must have malfunctioned again," Ben said. "We're five years late!"

Adams ignored the gumshoes' exchange. "That mercenary cut off the tusks and sold them," he said in an angry tone. "Then he left the carcass to

the locals, who fed the meat to their dogs. Wolves and other wild animals ate the rest."

"Gross," said Maya. "But I don't get it. Isn't this mammoth thousands of years old? How could the meat still be fresh?"

Adams smiled. "The ice, my dear. It kept the mammoth in a deep freeze all these years." He sighed. "At least the skeleton is mostly intact. It will take hard work, but I will make sure this great beast's remains rest in a museum."

"Thanks for your help," Ben said. Adams nodded and walked back toward the crew.

"Well, we missed Carmen's agent—by five years," Ben said. "We may as well go back to the Chronoskimmer." He grinned. "Unless you want to see if Adams will fix us a juicy mammoth-meat sandwich before we go!"

Maya made a face. "Ugh. No way. I don't care if it was preserved in ice for thousands of years. . . ." Her voice drifted off, and her eyes got a faraway look. "That's it. Ice! If ice is so good at preserving mammoths, maybe it's good at preserving clues, too. Let's take a look around."

Maya and Ben split up and searched the grounds near the mammoth. Suddenly Ben cried out, "Maya, you were right! Come here!"

Maya rushed to Ben's side. Ben pointed to the frozen river. About six inches below the ice was a sheet of paper with writing on it—in English, not Russian.

"'Here's one more piece in our little game. When did the dinosaur get its name?'" Maya read aloud.

"I know what it means!" Ben shouted. "A British scientist coined the name 'dinosaur' in 1841. I think his name was Owen—Richard Owen."

Maya jumped up. "Thank goodness you went through that dinosaur phase! Let's get back to the Chronoskimmer. I only hope we can beat V.I.L.E. to the scene this time."

"Maybe we can," Ben said. "I have a plan."

6

Plymouth, England,
August 1, 1841

"Let's hear it," Maya said, eager to know what Ben had in mind.

"What if we got there *before* the V.I.L.E. agent is supposed to rendezvous with Carmen?" Ben suggested.

"That's a brilliant idea!" Maya said. She could see it now: They would get there early—by maybe a day or two—and catch Carmen and her hench-person red-handed!

Maya was so excited, she started to run back to the Chronoskimmer. As she raced along, the cold wind stung her cheeks.

Ben started running too. "Race you!" he shouted when he reached her side. Maya moved forward with a burst of speed, but Ben soon caught up. They reached the Chronoskimmer at the same time.

"Good race," Maya said, panting. "Hey, Ben, you mentioned this scientist, Richard Owen, was British, but you didn't say where he lived. Do you know?"

Ben paused for a moment to catch his breath. "Well, I know that it was during a speech he gave that he first named the dinosaurs—'dinosauria' was what he actually called them."

"When was the speech given?" Maya wanted to know. "And where?"

"I—I can't remember," Ben said.

"Let's go inside," Maya said. "Maybe the Chronoskimmer can help."

Once inside the Chronoskimmer, Ben sat down in front of the control panel and started working. "'Richard Owen gave his speech at the annual meeting of the British Association for the Advancement of Science on August 2, 1841, in Plymouth, England,'" he read.

"That must be the date for the rendezvous," Maya said. "Although I am a bit disappointed."

Ben looked at her. "What are you talking about? We figured out the place. What's wrong?"

"Well, when you said that Owen was from

England, I was sort of hoping we'd be going to Oxford. I mean, Owen was an academic," Maya said. "So I thought that we were going to be able to pose as students at Oxford. It's my dream to study there one day, you know."

"Well, dream on," Ben said. "Besides, they didn't let girls study there in 1841!"

Maya sighed. "Well, I guess we'd better set our temporal coordinates for August 1, 1841," she said. "That way we'll beat Carmen and her hench-person there."

Ben nodded. He punched in the spatial and temporal coordinates. The time machine landed with a soft thump.

"Check out all those cool ships!" Ben said as they stepped outside.

Maya looked to where Ben was pointing. Several large sailboats with tall wooden masts sat in the water.

"Plymouth *is* a famous port, after all, Ben," Maya said. "It's no wonder there are a lot of ships out there."

Ben sat down on a rock and gazed out at the water.

"Did you know that Plymouth is where the *Mayflower* set sail from?" Maya asked.

Ben nodded his head, lost in thought.

"A lot of other people set sail from Plymouth too." Maya continued, reading from a printout: "'By 1295, Plymouth was an important naval base. Edward the First built and launched his ships for the Bordeaux wars here. In 1528 the explorer William Hawkins set sail to Brazil from Plymouth, and in 1577 Sir Francis Drake set out to sail the world, leaving Plymouth on November fifteenth, and—'"

Just then a boy in a cap and a heavy jacket ran past them. His foot got caught on one of the rocks, and he tripped and tumbled to the ground.

Maya walked over and bent down to give the boy a hand. But as soon as she reached out her hand to him, he scrambled to his feet and bolted away.

"Do I look that scary?" Maya wondered out loud. Just then she realized that something had brushed off the boy's jacket onto her hand. It felt cold and wet. Maya looked at her hand closely.

Snowflakes. How had the boy gotten snow on his jacket? After all, it was a sunny day, and there wasn't any snow on the ground. Unless . . .

"Hey!" Maya shouted. "That was no boy. That was Carmen's agent! She must have just gotten here from Siberia!"

"What did you say?" Ben asked, snapping out of his daze.

Maya took off after the agent. Ben followed her over the rocks, the salty air stinging his eyes. He had no idea where she was going, but he wasn't about to be left behind.

They were heading toward a lighthouse. Maya ran up to the stone tower and went inside.

"Maya!" Ben shouted. "Where are you?"

"I'm . . . right here," Maya panted. "It's . . . the agent! She went this way."

Ben followed Maya up a steep and winding stairway. The stairs were so rickety that he had to hold on to the cold stone wall for balance. "Maya— wait up!" Ben called. His voice echoed through the stairway.

"We missed her!" Ben heard Maya cry out.

Ben rushed up the rest of the stairs. He found Maya in the observatory. "Look!" she said, pointing below.

Ben looked outside too, and saw a figure clad in a winter jacket shimmying down a rope to the ground. It was the agent, all right, and there was no way they were going to catch up with her now.

"We were so close!" Maya said, smacking her fist into her hand.

Suddenly they heard the sound of footsteps. "Could it be . . ." Maya started, turning around. But it was not the agent. It was a young boy about seven years old.

The boy's eyes widened. "Another girl in trousers!" he cried. "And yours are short! I don't believe my eyes."

"Trousers?" Maya repeated. She looked down at her shorts.

"Yes, trousers," the boy said again. "Are you going to play croquet, by any chance?"

Maya thought fast. "Yes, yes I am. I mean, why else would I be wearing trousers?"

The boy smiled smugly. "I thought so. It's too odd otherwise. But that's not what the other girl said."

"The other girl?" Maya inquired.

"The one who was here right before you," the boy said. "I asked her if she was setting off to play croquet, and she said that she had never heard of the game. Imagine that—she had never heard of croquet!"

"Look!" Ben shouted. He had taken a pair of binoculars out of his backpack and was staring at something. "There she is again!"

Maya ran over to Ben's side. He handed her the binoculars. Sure enough, there was the agent. She

had her back to them, and she was talking to a man in a black cape. He wore a red flower in his lapel.

"Let's go!" Maya shouted, pulling Ben's arm. The two headed for the stairway. "Nice meeting you!" Maya called back to the boy, who looked very confused.

When Maya and Ben reached the ground, they ran down the street, frantically searching for the man with the red flower in his lapel. Finally they found who they were looking for.

"Excuse me, sir," Ben said.

The man turned around to face them, and Maya jumped back a little. He was a very intense-looking man. He was tall and thin, and had a big forehead. His wide mouth was drawn into a thin, straight line. His chin was large and imposing. Looking at that stern face, Maya wondered if he ever smiled.

"You must be the two American students I was looking for," the man said. "The students who are going to take notes at my speech tomorrow. Although I must confess, I was expecting two *boys*." He didn't sound happy at all.

The man thought she and Ben were his students! Maya realized. If they kept up this cover, they might have a chance to learn about his connection to Carmen's agent. Maya cleared her throat. "Oh, you

69

won't be disappointed, sir," she said.

"It's getting late," the man said. "I suppose you should spend the night with me. We'll sup on meat and potatoes. And then first thing in the morning we'll get to work. How does that sound?"

"Fine, sir," Ben said. "I have just one question. Who was that woman you were just talking to?"

The man shrugged. "She asked me if I was Richard Owen. And when I said yes, she asked me if she could make an appointment to see me tomorrow after my speech. Hmph! The *nerve* of that woman, being so bold!"

Richard Owen? Ben thought. They had struck paydirt!

In the morning, feeling well rested, Maya and Ben joined Richard Owen. He was bent over a desk, studying some papers.

"It's about time you two woke up!" Richard Owen snapped. "I need you to organize my papers! This is an important day for me, a most important day!"

Maya and Ben rushed to his side.

Ben picked up one of the papers and started reading. Richard Owen quickly snatched it from his hands. "There is no time for you to read, lad!" he shouted.

"I'm sorry, sir," Ben said. "I was just interested in—"

"What!" Owen interrupted. "Ancient creatures that roamed Earth long ago? The dinosauria, those terrible lizards—"

"Actually," Ben broke in, "scientists believe dinosaurs to be more closely related to birds."

"Do you dare to contradict me?" Owen said harshly.

Maya pulled Ben away. He couldn't give Owen this information. If he did, he could alter history! She had to change the subject as quickly as possible.

"Uh, sir," Maya started. "What time did you say you were meeting with that woman you ran into yesterday?"

"I *didn't* say." Richard Owen glared at Maya. "But that doesn't matter now. She's gone."

"Gone!" Maya and Ben said together.

"She was just here a moment ago. But as soon as she heard your footsteps, she ran out of here. It was most unusual," Owen said.

Ben and Maya stared at each other in shock. They'd been tricked!

"What did she say?" Ben asked.

Owen sighed heavily. "Really, I have no time for this!"

71

"Please sir, it's important," Maya said.

"Very well, if it will keep you quiet," Owen said. "I brought some bones with me here to Plymouth." Owen pointed to a box. "She asked if she could examine them. I agreed, if she promised to be careful."

Maya's heart raced. They may have been tricked, but they weren't licked yet. "Sir, may we take a look at the bones?" she asked cautiously.

Owen sighed again. "I suppose so. But don't disturb anything!"

Ben and Maya looked into the crate. The large grayish bones all looked the same, except for one. It was smaller and much whiter. It felt very light— almost like it was made out of plastic! Ben slipped the bone into his pocket. "Do you mind if Maya and I have some breakfast?" he asked.

"Hurry up," Richard Owen said. "There's a lot of work to be done!"

Maya followed Ben outside. He handed the plastic bone to Maya. "Check this out. It's a fake! Carmen's agent must have left it behind in her rush to leave," Ben said.

Maya peered at it. "Hey—it's hollow! And look what's inside," she said, pulling out a piece of paper.

She unrolled the paper and read: "'Little Jack

Horner sat in a corner, digging for dinos all day. Along came a mother who sat down beside him and frightened poor Jackie away.' "

"A *nursery rhyme*?" Ben said in disbelief.

Maya shook her head. "I'm stumped," she said.

"Wait a second," Ben said. "Jack Horner is a famous paleontologist. He dug up fossils of baby dinosaurs and nests in Choteau, Montana. I think around the year 1978."

"*Around* 1978?" Maya asked. "We've got to have a better date than that. We can't just go running all over the 1970s."

"I've got it! Horner is the guy who made a big discovery that led him to believe that dinosaurs took care of their babies in their nests. Let's go back to the Chronoskimmer and find the exact date."

"Well, I guess we know where and when we're headed next," Maya said. "At least our clothes will be more in style!"

Ben laughed, and followed her back to the Chronoskimmer.

7
Choteau, Montana, August 12, 1978

"**B**efore we go," Maya said, once they were back in the Chronoskimmer, "I think we should review what we have learned so far. We picked up some good clues and information."

Ben nodded and sat down to listen to her.

"First of all, I can't believe that Carmen and her henchperson *beat* us to Plymouth. I mean, that was such a brilliant plan, getting there early. Oh, well." Maya sighed.

"But we can cross Rosa Sarrosa-Arroz off our list of possible henchpeople," she continued, "because according to the boy in the lighthouse, the agent he met had never heard of croquet. And we know from Rosa's dossier that croquet is her hobby, so I guess she's out."

Ben typed this information into the Chrono-skimmer's control panel.

"So that leaves us with Katherine Drib and Dinah Sore," Maya concluded.

"I think we should call in for a warrant now," Ben said. "I'm sure Dinah Sore's our person. I mean, she's a dinosaur expert and everything! Doesn't it make sense?"

"She's still only a possible suspect," Maya reminded him. "But as I said before, we have to wait until we have some real proof before we get our warrant."

Ben knew Maya was right. But he had a feeling that Dinah Sore was the agent Carmen was leaving the clues for, and he just hoped his hunch panned out.

"Now let's get some information on this place we're headed to next," Maya said. "Choteau, Montana."

"'Choteau, Montana,'" Ben read from the printout he had gotten from the Chronoskimmer, "'is in an area known as the Two Medicine formation, which is a two-thousand-foot-thick wedge of sandstone, shale, and mudstone. The surface of the Two Medicine formation covers three thousand, six hundred square miles, running from the Canadian border in the north to Augusta, Montana, in the south, and from the Rocky Mountains in the west to the town of Choteau in the east.'"

"Uh, Ben," Maya interrupted. "Did you say sandstone, shale, and mudstone?"

"Yes. Why?"

"Because I don't think my sneakers are going to hold up." Maya wiggled her big toe through a hole in her shoe. "I think all that time travel proved to be a little too much wear and tear."

"Well, what can we do?" Ben wanted to know. "We can't go back to ACME Headquarters and change our *shoes*. That *T. rex* has probably destroyed it by now!"

Maya nodded. After a minute, she said, "I know! What if we go back to ACME a week before the *T. rex* appeared? Then we'll be able to get what we want, no problem!"

"Great idea!" Ben shouted. He punched the coordinates into the Chronoskimmer's control panel, and before they knew it, they were headed back home.

"I don't recall summoning you two," The Chief said sternly to Maya and Ben when they walked into her office.

"You didn't," Maya answered.

"This is a little hard to explain, Chief, but we're here on a mission from the future," Ben said.

"Is that so?" The Chief responded. "Well, gumshoes, I really don't have any time for your nonsense. I've got work to do."

Brriing! Brriing! rang the telephone on The Chief's desk. "Chief here," she said, picking up the receiver. "Hello—Maya?" Stunned, The Chief slowly pulled the phone from her ear. She stared at it, then back at Maya.

"What's going on here?" Maya whispered to Ben. "How can that be me on the phone? I'm here!"

"It's the rules of time travel," Ben whispered back. "The Chief is talking to the Maya from her present— our past. You're from her future—our present. There's another Ben walking around somewhere too."

Maya rubbed her head. "I told you this stuff makes my head hurt."

The Chief loudly slammed down the phone. She stared at Maya strangely. "Is this some kind of joke, gumshoes?"

"No, Chief," Ben said. "We really are from the future—a week into the future. You sent us on a mission in the Chronoskimmer."

"How do you know about the Chronoskimmer?" The Chief asked. "It's top secret. Besides, it's not ready for operation yet."

Ben rolled his eyes. "No kidding. This hasn't been an easy trip so far."

"Ben!" Maya cried. She couldn't believe he was joking at a time like this. She turned to The Chief. "We're telling the truth. ACME is in trouble. We need some help with this mission."

The Chief rubbed her eyes. "I'm not sure whether I should believe you or not, but something tells me I should. After all, you did know about the Chronoskimmer, and that phone call . . . What do you need?"

"A change of clothes, water bottles, and new sneakers," Maya said.

"And something to eat," Ben added.

The Chief stood up and beckoned to Maya and Ben to follow her.

"That was weird!" Maya said once they were back in the Chronoskimmer with all their supplies.

"But maybe that's how she knew we were going on a time-machine mission," Ben said.

Maya gave him a puzzled look. "I don't understand."

"Remember when The Chief said that she had some sort of 'experience' that made her believe we'd be using the time machine?" Ben asked.

Maya nodded.

"Well, that experience was us—our visit. Don't you see?"

Maya crinkled her brow. "I think I understand. But what I *know* is that we have to get on with things. We have to stop Carmen before she gets that *T. rex* egg!"

Ben punched the coordinates for Choteau, Montana, into the Chronoskimmer's control panel, and once again they were spinning through time. They didn't have to go back so far this trip—only to 1978.

The Chronoskimmer landed a short time later. After securing the time machine in a safe place, Maya and Ben set off. As they walked along the gravel road, the hot August sun beat down on their heads. All around them was low grass and eroding hills, dotted with grazing cattle.

"During the Cretaceous Period, when our *T. rex* friend lived," Maya said, "this land was covered by an interior sea. Over millions of years, the sea rose and fell, leaving muck on the bottom that eventually turned to shale."

"That's very interesting, Maya, but this is 1978, and what I want to know is: What's going on over there?" Ben asked, pointing to a crowd of people.

"It looks like a news crew," Maya said as they drew closer. "But I wonder what a news crew is doing here?"

"I know," Ben said, taking Maya's hand and ducking past the camerapeople. "They're here to report on Jack Horner's big discovery. Come on, let's get closer.

"Jack Horner and his group are digging on the Peeble family's land. They believe they're going to find baby dinosaur fossils here," Ben explained to Maya when they had made it to the front of the crowd.

There they saw the paleontologists hard at work. They had dug down into the mudstone and separated out the dinosaur bones. Their tools—shovels and picks and hock hammers and ice picks—were caked with dirt.

"That's Jack Horner over there," Ben said, pointing to a man talking to a news reporter. Dark-haired but balding, he had a beard and glasses.

"And that's Bob Makela," Ben said, pointing to another man. Makela also had a beard, but his hair was lighter and streaked with gray.

"Okay, folks, we're done for the day," someone from the dig said when the interviews had ended.

The camera crews began to pack away their equipment.

"What do we do now?" Maya asked. "We can't just hang around here for the night."

"Let's hide behind those trees and wait," Ben suggested.

"For what?" Maya wanted to know.

"I know that Jack Horner used his friend Bob Makela's backyard as his makeshift laboratory," Ben said. "Let's wait here and follow them home."

Ben's plan worked perfectly, and they were soon hiding in Bob Makela's backyard, watching the paleontologists at work.

Maya pointed to two of them, who were working on a big chunk of rock. The rock looked like it was covered in a white crust.

"What's that?" Maya asked.

"It's a bone covered in a plaster cast," Ben explained. "Dinosaur bones can break easily—just like human bones. When scientists dig up large bones, they leave them buried in pieces of rock. Then they cover the rock with a plaster cast."

"Like when I fell off my bike and broke my

leg last summer?" Maya asked.

Ben nodded. "Uh-huh. The cast keeps the big bones from breaking. Then the bones are taken to a lab, like this one, and the plaster comes off, and then the paleontologists extract the fossils from the rock."

"What about small bones?" Maya asked.

"They're painted with shellac—kind of a clear, shiny paint," Ben explained. "The shellac keeps the small bones from crumbling and turning to dust."

"I get it," Maya said. "But what about—"

"Shhh!" Ben said. "You're about to witness the coolest thing!"

Maya and Ben watched as the men gently removed plaster from the bones. Then they used small power tools to wear away the rock. And there was an intact dinosaur bone—some sort of snout with nose holes.

"That's the skull of the new species of dinosaur they found!" Ben said, jumping up.

"Shhh!" Maya said. "They'll hear us!"

"This is an *amazing* discovery!" Ben whispered. "This is the first time anyone found a nest of baby dinosaurs. And these babies stayed in the nest while they were growing up. Horner and Makela are going to name that creature *Maiasaura peeblesorum*. *Peeblesorum* is the species name, which comes from the owners of the land on which the fossils were found, the Peebles. *Maiasaura* comes from the Greek and means 'good mother lizard.'"

"Do you think the fact that they're digging up *baby* dinosaurs has something to do with Carmen stealing an egg from a mother *T. rex*?" Maya asked Ben. "I mean, it's an awfully big coincidence."

"Stop her! Thief!" someone yelled out before Ben could answer. Heavy footsteps came pounding right toward Ben and Maya's hiding place.

Just then, Maya and Ben saw a blurred form pass before their eyes. "The agent!" they shouted simultaneously.

"Let's go!" Maya yelled, pulling Ben to his feet.

"Stop those kids! They're probably accomplices!" a voice yelled. Maya and Ben gave each other panicked looks. They started running in different directions.

Maya turned left and scooted around a tree.

"They're getting away with valuable fossils!" someone else cried out.

Maya knew they had to get out of there—if she and Ben were caught, how would they explain what they were doing?

Suddenly Maya heard a soft thud. Then she heard Ben's muffled voice. "Keep going, Maya. Don't stop! Go on without me! You have to save—"

Don't stop? Go on? Maya thought. But Ben was in trouble! There was no way she was going to leave him alone in the 1970s. Wasn't that the decade of disco? Yuck!

Oof! Maya tripped over a shovel and fell to the ground. The next thing she knew, a burlap sack was tossed over her head and the world went dark.

8
Mongolia,
July 17, 1923

"**H**ey, get me out of here!" Maya cried. She ripped the scratchy bag off her head, spitting out dirt in the process.

A young man with a crew cut glared at her intently. Another man was holding Ben by the collar of his T-shirt.

"We saw you lurking around the lab," the man with the crew cut said. "You two have some explaining to do. Don't they, Lou?"

"They sure do, Joe," said the man holding Ben.

Maya and Ben exchanged glances. The agent must be long gone by now. They had to get back on her trail, fast.

"We don't know what you're talking about,"

Maya said. "We're just kids."

"Two very suspicious-looking kids," Lou said.

The man with the dark hair and glasses walked up to them. The man with lighter hair was by his side.

"What's going on here?" asked the dark-haired man.

"There's been a theft, Jack," Lou told him. "And I think these kids are involved."

"Yeah, a valuable fossil has been stolen," Joe chimed in.

The other man laughed. "That wasn't a fossil! That was a hard-boiled egg. I was going to eat it for dinner." He turned to Maya and Ben. "I'm sorry about all this. I'm Bob Makela. This is my friend Jack Horner." He pointed to the man with dark hair.

"It's nice to meet you," Maya said, rising to her feet. She spit out some more dirt. "Well, sort of."

Ben spoke up. "I'm Ben, and this is Maya. We're just visiting some friends of ours. We heard about the dig here and we really love dinosaurs, so we thought we'd come check it out."

Maya nodded. "That's right."

Bob Makela smiled. "I guess there's no harm done. I'm sorry about my friends here—they get a little carried away sometimes."

Lou and Joe looked down at their feet sheepishly.

Jack Horner laughed. "This is all pretty funny," he said. "It looked like we had a major thief on our hands. But all we had was a *Velociraptor*."

"A veloci-*what*?" Maya asked.

"That's just Jack's sense of humor," Makela said. "A *Velociraptor* is a dinosaur that steals other dinosaur's eggs. The name means 'egg-seizer.'"

Ben and Maya looked at each other. "Maybe it's a clue!" Ben whispered to Maya.

Maya turned to the two paleontologists. "Can you tell us some more about the *Velociraptor*?" she asked.

"Sure," Jack Horner said. "In 1923, Roy Chapman Andrews led an expedition to look for fossils in the Gobi Desert in Mongolia. He and his crew uncovered several nests of the first dinosaur eggs ever found. They found a skeleton of a small dinosaur crouching over one of the nests. Scientists thought the dinosaur was trying to steal the eggs, so it was named *Velociraptor*."

"No one's ever really proven that theory," Makela cut in. "But it's a pretty good guess."

Ben stared at the men in awe. "It must be so

cool to study dinosaurs all the time. You guys seem to know everything."

"Not everything," Horner said with a laugh. "But we'd be happy to show you around the lab if you'd like."

"Great!" Ben said, but Maya grabbed his sleeve.

"Thanks for the offer," Maya said. "But we've really got to go. We're kind of anxious to get somewhere."

Ben sighed. "Yeah, she's right. But thanks anyway!"

The men nodded, and headed back to their lab. Ben and Maya ran back to the Chronoskimmer.

"You've got to admit that Carmen's agent is pretty clever," Ben said. "The world's *greatest* egg stealer is leading us to the world's *first* egg stealer."

"We've got her this time," Maya said. She typed furiously into the Chronoskimmer's data finder. "There's a lot of interesting data on Andrews and the *Velociraptor*. It says here Andrews was an explorer who was the Indiana Jones of his time. A real colorful character."

Ben rolled his eyes. "I've met enough colorful characters for one day!"

Maya ignored him and scrolled down the computer screen. "Andrews set up camp near the

Flaming Cliffs of Shabarakh Usu in Mongolia. The first big discovery was a nest of fossilized eggs, which was made on July thirteenth, 1923. It says here that the *Velociraptor* was discovered a few days later."

"Let's try July seventeenth," Ben suggested. "That's my dad's birthday."

"Why not?" Maya said. "At least we know exactly where to look this time. We should be able to land right next to Andrews's tent!" She punched the spatial and temporal coordinates into the keyboard.

"Uh, Maya, maybe that's not such a good idea," Ben said. "How are we going to explain a giant silver box landing in the middle of the Gobi Desert?"

Maya grinned sheepishly. "Sorry, Ben," she said as the Chronoskimmer took off. "We'll think of something when we get there."

Maya was still thinking when she and Ben cautiously opened the Chronoskimmer's door—and walked right into a man wearing a khaki shirt and shorts. A wide-brimmed hat shaded his face from the bright desert sun.

"The Chronoskimmer! What a lovely surprise!" A wide smile lit up the man's deeply tanned face. "And you two are ACME agents, I presume?"

"We're gumshoes, actually," Maya said. "But

how do you know about the Chronoskimmer? And ACME?"

"Yeah," Ben said. "And who are you, anyway?"

"I'm Roy Chapman Andrews," the man replied. "As for the rest of your questions, let's get out of the desert sun and I'll explain everything."

Maya and Ben followed Andrews to a row of blue tents. The tents sat on the sand next to a long ridge of rocks. The rocks glowed a deep red in the sunlight.

"Wow," Maya said, taking in the scene. "This must be why they call them the Flaming Cliffs."

"Good guess," Ben replied. "This place is cool."

"Cool? My boy, it's over a hundred degrees today!" Andrews exclaimed. "I'd better get you out of the sun without delay."

Andrews led Maya and Ben into a nearby tent. A small table covered with papers was against one of the tent's walls. Two low stools, two cots, and some folded blankets filled the rest of the small structure.

Andrews gestured toward the stools. "Please, please, sit down," he said. "Let me explain everything to you."

The gumshoes sat down and looked at him expectantly.

"It's all really quite simple," Andrews said. "I'm one of ACME's special time agents. A few months ago The Chief paid me a visit in the Chronoskimmer and told me of ACME's valiant fight to keep the world safe from the thieving Carmen Sandiego. She told me she was recruiting agents in different time periods to aid ACME in this fight. I gladly accepted her invitation."

"Of course!" Maya said. "That explains it."

"But I have some questions for the two of you," Andrews said. "As ACME time travelers, why weren't you told about the existence of the time agents? And what are you doing here?"

"I think I know," Ben said. "We're the first ones ever to use the Chronoskimmer. When we began our mission, The Chief hadn't yet had a chance to use the Chronoskimmer to recruit the time agents."

"I get it," Maya said. "She's going to recruit the time agents after we get back."

"As for your second question," Ben said. "That's a long story. . . ."

Maya tapped her foot impatiently as Ben told Andrews the whole story of their adventure through time.

"Fascinating tale," Andrews said when Ben had

finished. "It reminds me of the time I was exploring the jungles of—"

"Sorry to interrupt you, Mr. Andrews," Maya said. "But we really need to get back on the case."

Andrews nodded. "Certainly. I understand." He stood up, his head grazing the ceiling of the tent. "I think I have some information that may help you. Follow me."

Ben and Maya shielded their eyes from the bright desert sun. Andrews led them to a larger tent a few feet away.

Inside the tent, a small man with a white mustache was working behind a long table. The table was covered with piles of bones and small groups of large, round fossils.

"Dinosaur eggs!" Maya exclaimed.

"That's correct," Andrews said. "And this is the man who discovered them, George Olsen."

Olsen was brushing desert sand off a small clutch of three eggs. He looked up at Maya and Ben, his eyes widening in surprise. "Good heavens, Andrews, where did these children come from?"

"I'm afraid that information is top secret, George," Andrews said. "But they do need your help. I was hoping you could tell them about yesterday's incident."

Olsen laughed. "I've never had so much excitement in my life as when I signed on with you, Roy," he said. "Yesterday's incident certainly was strange. It was early morning, and I was walking into this tent, only to bump into a strange woman. She had a cap pulled over her eyes, and I thought it might be one of the cooks on our expedition."

"Was it?" Maya asked.

Olsen shook his head. "No, it wasn't. You see, the woman was carrying a dinosaur egg, but it didn't appear to be fossilized. The shell was covered with brown specks, and it was shiny. When I started to question her about it, she ran off. I ran after her, but I lost sight of her quickly—almost as if she disappeared." Olsen held up a gray wool cap. "This is all she left behind. It fell off her head as she ran."

"Did you get a good look at her face?" Ben asked.

"No, I didn't," Olsen said. "It all happened so fast."

Maya turned to Andrews. "That must have been Carmen's agent! She was probably here to pick up another clue from Carmen."

"If that's true, then we've missed her," Ben

said. "Did she leave anything behind besides her hat? Weren't there any other clues?"

"Nothing," Olsen said.

"I can vouch for that," Andrews said. "After I heard about the incident, I thought it was worth investigating. Our crew combed the area. We couldn't find anything."

"It's hopeless!" Ben cried.

"Maybe not," Maya said. She pulled a hair from inside the hat. "This hair is brown, all the way down to the root. Dinah Sore is a natural blonde. That means—"

"That's means that the agent is Katherine Drib!" Ben interrupted.

Maya smiled. "We've got enough evidence to get a warrant now! Isn't that great?"

Ben's shoulders drooped. "Not really," he said. "We might be able to get a warrant, but without more clues, we don't know where to look next. It looks like Carmen's beat us again!"

Drat! How could Drib be so careless? She's never been able to keep her head on straight, much less her hat.

Not that it matters. Without any clues, those ACME amateurs are lost. While they're stuck scratching their heads in the Gobi Desert, I'll be on my way to pick up my prehistoric prize—and complete the greatest theft of all time!

9
Acme Headquarters, San Francisco, June 1, 1985

"**W**e can't give up now!" Maya said. She and Ben were back in the Chrono-skimmer, and Maya was pounding away at the keyboard again. "There's got to be something we missed."

"Look under '*Velociraptor*,'" Ben suggested.

"One second," Maya said. "Here it is. Most of the information repeats what Horner and Makela told us. But there is one thing . . ."

Ben peered over her shoulder. "What is it?"

"It says here that in 1993 scientists went back to Mongolia. They found *Velociraptors* near nests of eggs again," Maya read. "But this time they realized the *Velociraptors* weren't eating the eggs at all—they were hatching from the eggs!"

"So *Velociraptors* had a bad name all those years," Ben said. "That's terrible. Do you think it's a clue?"

Maya shrugged. "I'm not sure. It's not like Carmen to set up a rendezvous in the same country twice in a row."

"That's true," Ben said. "But it's all we've got to go on."

"Maybe so," Maya agreed. "But before we check it out, why don't we go back to ACME and get a warrant for Katherine Drib? If we *are* right, we'll be prepared."

"Good idea," Ben said. "But let's go back to the present this time. I think we've scared The Chief enough already."

Maya nodded. "I'd rather face that *T. rex* again!"

She programmed the Chronoskimmer, and the time machine took off again. But this time, instead of a whirring sound, Maya and Ben heard loud clanks and creaks.

"Yikes!" Maya cried. "This doesn't sound too good."

"Maybe the Chronoskimmer's getting tired," Ben said. He patted the console gently. "Come on, you can do it!"

Maya and Ben braced themselves for the Chronoskimmer's landing. The machine touched down with a loud thud.

Ben cautiously opened the door. They were in the agents' room at ACME Headquarters. The lights were off, and the moon shone through the large windows.

"It's quiet," Ben remarked.

"Too quiet," Maya said. "Where's the *T. rex*? And why isn't the building in a shambles right now?"

Ben was staring at a nearby bulletin board. "I think I know," he said. He pointed to a calendar. It read JUNE 1985.

Maya groaned. "We're years too early! The Chronoskimmer must have malfunctioned. What a surprise!" she said sarcastically.

Ben sighed. "I guess we'll have to try again."

"Not just yet," Maya said, her voice rising. "There's something you've got to see."

She walked to one of the ACME agent's desks and switched on the desk lamp. The light illuminated a black-and-white nameplate. The name shone in the yellow light: CARMEN SANDIEGO.

Ben gasped. "It's Carmen's desk! She used to be an ACME agent, remember?"

"Before she turned to a life of crime," Maya said. "Ben, we can't pass up this chance. There might be something here that will give us a clue about how Carmen operates."

Ben was already rummaging through the desk drawers. "I found something!" he cried. He held up a small black notebook. "It looks like her journal."

Maya opened the book. "Here's her latest entry," she said.

Ben started to read out loud: "'June 1, 1985. Took a test run in the Chronoskimmer today. Thyme was nervous, as usual, but I convinced him. He was right about one thing—that machine needs a lot of work. I tried to go ten years into the past, to June 1, 1975, but I ended up ten years in the future. It was almost midnight, and I was in the American Museum of Natural History in New York. At least I think it was the museum—the dinosaur exhibit looked completely different from what it looks like today.

"'But the strangest moment came when I saw a woman in a red coat and hat come running past me. At first I thought it was odd, because the museum was closed. Then I noticed that the

woman was carrying a large egg with brown speckles. I tried to stop her to question her about it, and for a split second we locked eyes. I was shocked.

" 'It was me! I was looking right at myself. Was I encountering myself in the future? What an intriguing possibility. Before I could ask her—I mean me—I—I mean she—had disappeared.

" 'As I took the Chronoskimmer back to ACME, one thought dominated my mind: I look wonderful in the color red. . . .' "

"Ben!" Maya cried. "Do you know what this means?"

"I think so," Ben said. "When Carmen saw herself in the future, she caught herself right after she got the egg from the agent!"

"It makes sense," Maya said. "The American Museum of Natural History revamped its dinosaur exhibit in 1995. I remember, because Aunt Velma took me to see it. It was cool. They had a whole new exhibit about the *T. rex*."

Ben ran to the Chronoskimmer. "According to the computer, the new *T. rex* exhibit opened on June 2, 1995. Carmen wrote that she was trying to get back to June 1, 1975, but she ended up in the wrong year. She must have landed on June 1,

1995—the night before the exhibit opened!"

"That's got to be it!" Maya said. "We've found a clue after all. We'll solve this case yet."

"We sure will," Ben said. "Thanks to Carmen!"

10
New York City,
June 1, 1995

"**N**ew York City, here we come!" Maya
shouted.

"Wait a minute," Ben said. "We still need that
warrant for Drib."

"We'd have to take the Chronoskimmer into
the future," said Maya. "And since it's been mal-
functioning, I don't want to use it any more than
we have to."

Ben looked at the Chronoskimmer's control
panel. "I've got it! Why don't we just send an E-
mail into the future," he said. He typed: REQUEST
WARRANT FOR ARREST OF KATHERINE DRIB. SUSPECTED
OF STEALING T. REX EGG FROM CRETACEOUS PERIOD.

"Will this work?" Maya asked nervously.

Ben shrugged. "I hope so."

The control panel began to hum, and a few seconds later a crisp piece of paper slid into Ben's hands.

"It's the warrant!" Ben said.

"Then let's go!" Maya said. Her hands flew to the keyboard: SPATIAL COORDINATES: AMERICAN MUSEUM OF NATURAL HISTORY, NEW YORK CITY. TEMPORAL COORDINATES: JUNE 1, 1995, 11:30 P.M.

The machine began to rattle and shake violently. The lights on the control panel flashed.

Maya grabbed on to a wall for support. "I think the Chronoskimmer's a little tired from all this time traveling!" she shouted over the noise.

"I just hope we make it!" Ben shouted back.

As suddenly as it began, the shaking came to a halt and the flashing lights shut off.

"We must have landed," Maya said.

Ben walked to the door. "I hope we're in the right place—and the right time."

He opened the door and peered out. "Uh, Maya," he started, "isn't the museum in the *city*?"

Maya nodded. "Yes. It's in Manhattan, on West Seventy-ninth Street and Central Park West," she answered, reading from the printout.

"Well, this isn't exactly the city," Ben said,

pointing outside. "I mean, I was expecting to see *skyscrapers,* not *trees."*

Maya laughed. "That's because we've landed in Central Park," she explained. "Don't worry, the museum is right across the street." She opened the Chronoskimmer's door and stepped outside.

"Don't!" Ben shouted.

Maya jumped back inside. Ben looked as pale as a ghost. "What's wrong, Ben?" Maya asked, wondering what had frightened her friend.

"Maya," Ben began. "It's eleven thirty at night. We're in the middle of a huge park in a huge city. It's *dangerous*!" he shouted. "You've heard the stories, haven't you?"

Maya couldn't believe her ears. Ben, afraid? "Ben, what's your problem? I mean, after all we've been through. We've even been chased by a dinosaur—what could be scarier than that?"

"But I've read stories about all the crime in this park," Ben said.

"We'll be okay, Ben. We're right by a park entrance," Maya replied.

Ben sighed. "You're right. I guess I'm just a little jumpy. Come on. Let's go catch that thief."

Maya and Ben quickly reached the street, which was buzzing with activity. Yellow taxicabs zigzagged down the avenue, and groups of people walked along the sidewalk.

Maya looked at the street signs: Central Park West and West Seventy-fourth Street. "Come on, Ben," she said. "The museum is just five blocks uptown, on Seventy-ninth."

As they walked along, Maya filled Ben in on some of the museum's history. " 'The American Museum of Natural History is the largest natural-history museum in the world. Its thirty-nine permanent exhibits and three special halls represent just a small part of the museum's thirty million artifacts and specimens.' "

Ben whistled in amazement.

" 'The museum has the world's largest collections of spiders, fossils, mammals, and whales,' " Maya continued. " 'One of the most popular exhibits is the ninety-four-foot-long blue whale skeleton.' "

"And I bet the other most popular exhibits are the dinosaur halls," Ben added.

Maya nodded. "Look," she said. "We're here!"

Ben stared at the imposing structure. He took the printout from Maya and began to read: " 'The museum is housed in nineteen interconnected buildings on a twenty-three-acre quadrangle. The original building, a redbrick Victorian Gothic, was completed in 1874.' "

Ben stopped reading to look up at the museum. There was a big flight of stairs that led up to one of the building's entrances, but there was no doubt that at this late hour the doors would be locked. "I have just one question," Ben said. "How do we get in?"

"The same way Katherine Drib did," Maya said, pointing to a rope dangling out of the museum's second-story window.

"Of course!" Ben exclaimed. "Katherine Drib's hobby is mountain climbing. Do you think we can make it up there?"

"I don't think we have a choice," Maya said, taking two pairs of gloves out of her backpack and tossing one pair to Ben. "Put those on. They'll help us avoid rope burns."

"But what if someone sees us?" Ben asked. "There are tons of people around. What if one of them calls the police?"

"We'll deal with that when and if it happens," Maya said. "Right now, this is the only way in."

Maya gave Ben a boost, and he easily scurried up the rope. Luckily, there were places along the building where he could anchor his feet. As soon as Ben was up and through the window, Maya began her ascent. She soon joined her friend inside.

The museum's halls were eerily dark and quiet. "This way," Maya whispered. "I think I remember one of the dinosaur halls being over here."

Ben followed Maya down the hall. It was so quiet that he could swear he heard his heart beating. Suddenly Ben stopped short. A fifty-foot-tall *Barosaurus* was rearing up, protecting itself from an attacking *Allosaurus*! What an amazing sight!

"Wow!" Ben gasped. He quickly clasped his hands over his mouth.

Maya spun around to face him. "It's a pretty incredible exhibit, isn't it?" she whispered.

But Ben wasn't listening to her. He ducked under the red velvet rope in front of one of the exhibits to get a closer look.

"Ben," Maya whispered urgently. "You're not supposed to get that close. You could damage something."

"I'll be careful," Ben said. He took out his flashlight and shone it on the fossils. "I can't believe I've never been to this place before—it's *awesome*!"

"Especially after hours, when there's no security guard to drag you off," Maya said, pulling Ben away from the skeleton.

"Come on," she said. "We'll come back here another time, I promise. But right now we have to find Katherine Drib. We don't want to miss her rendezvous with Carmen."

Reluctantly Ben left the dinosaur's side.

"I don't think they're in this hall," Maya said after they had searched the place. "Where do you think those two would plan to meet?" She pulled out a map of the museum. "This must be it!" she exclaimed. "There's a *T. rex* exhibit on the fourth floor—let's go!"

Maya and Ben raced up the stairs to the fourth floor. "There it is!" Ben said. "The *T. rex*!"

"And there *she* is!" Maya said, pointing to a figure crouched next to the skeleton.

"Katherine Drib," Maya announced. "We have a warrant for your arrest."

The woman crouching under the *T. rex* stood up. "I'm just cleaning up," she replied in a frail, shaky voice. The woman was wearing a gray uniform, and her hair was covered with a gray bandanna. She was carrying a mop and a dust rag. A few feet away from her stood a cart with additional cleaning supplies.

"Sorry, wrong person," Ben said, leading Maya away. He lowered his voice to a whisper. "She could turn us in to a security guard. We'd better go."

Maya followed Ben reluctantly. Something wasn't quite right about that cleaning woman. She turned around for one more look. The woman rolled up her sleeves and started mopping the floor.

Maya gasped. The cleaning woman had a tattoo of an eagle on her left biceps.

Just like Katherine Drib!

"It's her!" Maya cried. She ran for the cart. Katherine Drib tried to reach the cart first.

"The egg!" Maya shouted. "She's got it, Ben! We've got to get it away." Maya made a flying leap and landed on the cart. Maya and the cart rolled down the hall.

Katherine Drib was right on her heels. *She's gaining on me*, Maya thought. *Come on, think fast!* A bottle of cleaning fluid in the cart caught Maya's eye. That was it! She reached over and grabbed the bottle. She unscrewed the cap and poured some of the cleaning fluid on the floor.

She looked behind her. Katherine Drib was sliding all over the slippery liquid. Arms flailing, she tried to steady herself, but it was too late—her legs flew out from under her and she fell to the floor.

"Great work!" Ben shouted, rushing up to Drib.

"Katherine Drib," he said, pulling out the

warrant and his ACME badge, "you're under arrest."

"Now tell us exactly where Carmen is supposed to meet you," Maya said, climbing off the cart.

"You wouldn't arrest a little old lady, would you?" Drib said.

"Nice try," Maya said. "But we know who you are. It would be in your best interest to help us."

But Katherine Drib glared at them and didn't say a word. Ben pulled out some rope from his backpack and tied Drib's hands and feet to make sure she wouldn't get away.

Maya walked back over to the cart and gently lifted the dinosaur egg. Its brown, speckled shell shimmered in the dim light. "Well, we got two of the things we came here for—the egg and Drib. Now all we need is Carmen. Any suggestions?"

"I think the first thing we should do is put that egg in a safe place," Ben suggested. "We don't want Carmen to get her hands on it now." He looked around the hall. "How about where it belongs?" Ben pointed to the skeleton of a *T. rex*.

Maya shook her head. "Too obvious. How about putting it with another one?" she said, pointing to a different fossil.

"The *Ankylosaurus*," Ben said. "Perfect!"

Maya put the egg down gently. "Now all we've

got to do is sit here," she said, "and wait for Carmen. We're finally going to catch her!"

The white bones of the *T. rex* loomed above them as Maya and Ben waited in the quiet museum hall.

A sudden flash of light blinded them. As their eyes slowly came back into focus, they saw a figure clad in red gently balanced on top of the *T. rex* skeleton. The V.I.L.E. time machine sat next to the *T. rex* on the floor below.

"Carmen!" Maya cried. She couldn't believe how close she was to the world's most notorious criminal mastermind. She had been near her before, but Maya was sure there was no way Carmen would escape her grasp this time.

"Carmen Sandiego—" Ben began.

"You're under arrest!" Maya finished. It felt so good to say those words.

Carmen just gave them a big smile. "You are two of the best detectives I've ever known," she said. "I've been impressed with you in the *past*." Carmen stopped to laugh at her little joke. "But I never thought you'd be able to keep up with the clues I left for Drib. Unfortunately, Drib was not up to this task!"

"I repeat," Maya said. "You're under arrest!"

"Ah, not this time, my little gumshoe," Carmen said. "You may have my agent and my egg—too bad it won't get a chance to hatch in the present. But you won't get me. Not now—not ever!"

With that, Carmen slid down the tail of the *T. rex*, and before Maya and Ben could say "dinosaur," she jumped into the time machine. There was another flash of light, and the machine disappeared.

"She escaped in her time machine!" Maya exclaimed. "We'll never find her now."

"I hate to admit it, but you're right," Ben said. "She could be anywhere in time."

Maya sighed. "Well, at least we got the egg. I say that before we go home, we return it to its rightful owner."

"What do we do with her?" Ben asked, pointing at Katherine Drib.

"She's coming along for the ride," Maya said. "After all, she's been there before."

11

Acme Headquarters, San Francisco, California, Present Day

"**G**ood detective work, gumshoes," The Chief told Maya and Ben back in her office. "Although I must confess I am a tad disappointed you didn't nab Carmen this time."

Maya sighed. She couldn't believe how close they had been, but once again Carmen had gotten away.

"At least we returned the egg," Ben offered.

"And the mother *T. rex* was a lot happier to see us this time," Maya added.

The Chief nodded. "Yes. Thanks to you two, ACME was saved. You were able to intercept Carmen, arrest her henchperson, and, most importantly, return the egg. Thankfully, that angry *T. rex* was never given the chance to destroy this place," she said, tapping on her desk. "If it weren't for you two and the Chronoskimmer, we wouldn't be sitting here now having this conversation."

Maya rubbed her head.

"Are you feeling okay, Maya?" The Chief asked.

"I'm sorry, Chief, but this time-travel stuff still gives me a headache," she said.

The Chief laughed. Maya was glad to see that The Chief was back to her old self. The last time they had seen her, she was tense and confused. But that was no wonder—so much weird stuff had gone on!

"It's really simple, Maya," Ben said. "Carmen sent Katherine Drib back in time to steal the dinosaur egg. The plan was to rendezvous with Carmen in the American Museum of Natural History and hand over the egg. Then Carmen would go off with the egg, and once it grew into a full-fledged *T. rex*, she would use it to destroy ACME Headquarters. The plan worked once—but not when we were able to travel back in time and stop it from happening."

"And Carmen left some good clues for her agent, which you two picked up on. She wasn't able to shake you for very long," The Chief said. "I must say I am very proud of you. Very proud."

Maya and Ben smiled.

"As a token of my appreciation, I have a little something for each of you. I know this goes against protocol, but seeing that this was a different kind of case, I think that a little bonus is in order." She pressed a buzzer and in walked Agent Thyme.

Maya and Ben exchanged glances. What was The Chief up to now?

Agent Thyme had an anguished look on his face. "So clever, so brilliant, so evil," he muttered.

"Agent Thyme!" The Chief snapped. "Haven't we heard enough for one day?"

"Sorry, Chief," he said, handing her two plain white envelopes.

"Agent Thyme and Yul B. Gowan have helped me arrange two very special trips for you," The Chief explained, handing Maya and Ben the envelopes.

Ben ripped open his envelope. "A behind-the-scenes tour of the American Museum of Natural History!" he exclaimed. "How did you know I've always wanted to explore that museum? I hear they've got a basement full of dinosaur bones. This is going to be great."

Maya opened her envelope. "I can't believe it!" she shouted, jumping out of her chair. "I'm going to study at Oxford! They're offering a special junior geography course there—and I'm going to be part of it! Thank you, Chief!"

The Chief smiled and nodded. Just then the phone on her desk rang. "Chief here," she said, picking it up. "Yes. Yes. Very interesting." She covered the mouthpiece and mumbled something into the phone, then hung up.

"That was a new case, gumshoes," The Chief began.

Maya's and Ben's faces fell. Another case so soon? What about their trips?

"But don't worry," The Chief said with a smile. "I told them that you two don't have the *time* right now!"